Usborne English Re

Starter Level

THE THREE BILLY GOATS

Retold by Mairi Mackinnon

Illustrated by Kyle Beckett

English language consultant: Peter Viney

Contents

3

The Three Billy Goats

16

Goats and other animals

17

Activities

22

Word list

You can listen to the story online here:
www.usborneenglishreaders.com/
threebillygoats

These three goats are brothers. Their names are Boris, Bert and Benny.

The word for boy goats is 'billy' goats. These are the Billy Goats Gruff.

The Billy Goats Gruff eat grass all day, but billy goats are always hungry.

There's not much grass here. It's all thin and yellow.

We need some new grass.

"Look!" says Benny, the little billy goat. "Look there! I can see lots of grass, lovely green grass and flowers."

"We can't go there," says Bert, the middle billy goat. "There's a bridge."

"What's wrong with the bridge?" asks Benny.

"There's a troll under that bridge," says Boris, the big billy goat.

Trolls EAT billy goats. Everyone knows that.

A few days later, Benny says, "It's no good. I can't eat this thin grass. I'm going up that hill."

"Be careful, Benny," say his brothers.

Benny walks on to the bridge.

His feet go tap, tap, tap.

Who's that tap-tap-tapping on my bridge?

The troll jumps on to the bridge.
He is big and green and ugly.

"Food!" he says. "Come here, food!"

"Wait!" says Benny. "Please don't
eat me. I'm very little."

I'm
hungry!

"My two big brothers are coming,"
says Benny. "Wait for them."

The troll looks at him. "You're right," he says. "You're very thin. I can see your bones. I need more food!" He goes back under the bridge.

Benny goes up the hill. There's lots of new green grass.

"Hey, brothers," he shouts. "This grass is really good. Come and try it!"

"Right," says Bert, the middle brother. "I'm going."

"Be very careful," says Boris.

Bert walks on to the bridge. His feet go tap, tap, tap.

Who's that tap-tap-tapping on my bridge?

The troll jumps on to the bridge.
"Food!" he says. "Come here, food!"
"Ooh, you *are* ugly," says Bert.
"I don't want to be your meal."
"I'm hungry!" says the troll.
"I understand," says Bert.

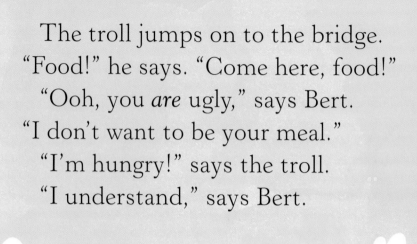

I'm hungry too.
Look at me. I'm all
bones. You don't want
to eat me.

"You need a good meal – a *big* meal. My big brother is coming. Wait for him."

"When is your big brother coming?" asks the troll.

"Soon, very soon," says Bert.

The troll goes back under the bridge, and Bert goes up the hill. "Hello, Benny," he says.

They shout to their brother, "Come here, Boris!"

"Don't eat all that grass," shouts Boris. "Wait for me!"

He walks on to the bridge. His feet go tap, tap, tap.

"Who's that tap-tap-tapping on my bridge?" says the troll. He jumps on to the bridge again.

"It's the big brother!" he says. "Come here, food!"

"What do you mean, *food*?" asks Boris. "*I'm* not your food."

I'm hungry. I want my food now!

The troll is big and ugly, but Boris is big and strong. He puts his head down and he runs at the troll. The troll flies off the bridge and falls down into the water.

SPLASH!

Boris goes up the hill. "Hello, Boris!" say his brothers. "Where's that troll?"

"He's back under the bridge, I think," says Boris.

Boris is right. "My head hurts," says the troll. "My back hurts. My legs hurt. I don't like goats!"

Boris and Bert and Benny eat the good green grass all day, every day. They never see the troll again.

Goats and other animals

There are goats in most countries in the world. Goats often live on farms. We get food and other things we need from animals on farms.

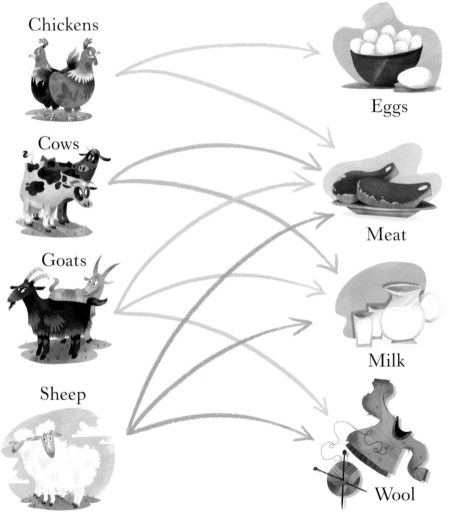

Chickens

Cows

Goats

Sheep

Eggs

Meat

Milk

Wool

Do these animals live on farms near you?
Do you know the names of other farm animals?

Activities

The answers are on page 24.

Can you see it in the picture?
Which three things *can't* you see?

bridge	goat	grass	hill
fish	road	flower	sun
sky	tree	troll	water

Where is everybody?

Can you say who is where in the picture below?

Benny   The troll   Some fish   A bird   Boris

1. .... is under the bridge.
2. .... is in the sky.
3. .... are in the water.
4. .... is on the bridge.
5. .... isn't in the picture.

What are they thinking?

Choose the right words.

What can
I hear?
Food?

You can't
stop me!

I can't eat
this grass.

1.

2.

3.

The end of the story

Choose the right words.

falls flies goes lives makes puts runs

Boris (1)........ his head down, and he
(2)........ at the troll. The troll (3)........
off the bridge and (4)........ down in
the water. Boris (5)........ up the hill.

That's better!

Which three sentences go with picture 1?
Which go with picture 2?

1.

A. The grass is lovely and green.

B. The goats are hungry.

C. The goats are happy.

2.

D. The grass is thin and yellow.

E. The goats need more grass.

F. There are trees and flowers.

Word list

bones (n pl) your bones are inside your body. They are hard and white.

bridge (n) a way over over a river, a train track or a road.

careful (adj) when something is dangerous or difficult, you need to be careful.

goat (n) a kind of animal, a little like a sheep. Goats eat grass and often live on farms.

grass (n) a green plant. There is grass almost everywhere in the world, on hills and in fields and gardens.

hill (n) a hill is high ground. A very big hill is a mountain.

goat

grass

shout (v) to say something very loudly. Sometimes people shout when they are angry. Sometimes you shout when someone is far away.

strong (adj) when you are strong, you can move or carry heavy things.

thin (adj) when people or animals don't eat enough, for a long time, they are thin. When grass doesn't grow much, it is thin.

troll (n) a kind of animal in stories. Trolls are ugly and not nice.

ugly (v) when something is ugly, it doesn't look nice, it looks bad.

ugly troll ----->

hill

Answers

Can you see it in the picture?
Three things you can't see:
road, sun, tree.

Where is everybody?
1. The troll
2. A bird
3. Some fish
4. Benny
5. Boris

What are they thinking?
1. I can't eat this grass.
2. What can I hear? Food?
3. You can't stop me!

The end of the story
1. puts
2. runs
3. flies
4. falls
5. goes

That's better!
1. B, D, E
2. A, C, F

You can find information about
other Usborne English Readers here:
www.usborneenglishreaders.com

Designed by Melissa Gandhi
Series designer: Laura Nelson Norris
Edited by Jane Chisholm

First published in 2019 by Usborne Publishing Ltd.,
Usborne House, 83-85 Saffron Hill, London EC1N 8RT, England.
www.usborne.com Copyright © 2019 Usborne Publishing Ltd.